A Note to Parents

For many children, learning math is difficult and "I hate math!" is their first response—to which many parents silently add "Me, too!" Children often see adults comfortably reading and writing, but they rarely have such models for mathematics. And math fear can be catching!

The easy-to-read stories in this **Hello Math** series were written to give children a positive introduction to mathematics and parents a pleasurable re-acquaintance with a subject that is important to everyone's life. **Hello Math** stories make mathematical ideas accessible, interesting, and fun for children. The activities and suggestions at the end of each book provide parents with a hands-on approach to help children develop mathematical interest and confidence.

Enjoy the mathematics!
• Give your child a chance to retell the story. The more familiar children are with the story, the more they will understand its mathematical concepts.
• Use the colorful illustrations to help children "hear and see" the math at work in the story.
• Treat the math activities as games to be played for fun. Follow your child's lead. Spend time on those activities that engage your child's interest and curiosity.
• Activities, especially ones using physical materials, help make abstract mathematical ideas concrete.

Learning is a messy process and learning about math calls for children to become immersed in lively experiences that help them make sense of mathematical concepts and symbols.

Although learning about numbers is basic to math, other ideas, such as identifying shapes and patterns, measuring, collecting and interpreting data, reasoning logically, and thinking about chance are also important. By reading these stories and having fun with the activities, you'll help your child enthusiastically say "**Hello, Math**," instead of "I hate math."

—Marilyn Burns
National Mathematics Educator
Author of *The I Hate Mathematics! Book*

For Luke and Lila, Justin and Ian
— A.S.

To my dear friends ... Bud & Evelyne Johnson
— L.D.

ISBN 0-590-26599-7

Copyright © 1995 by Scholastic Inc.
The activities on pages 27–32 copyright © 1995 by Marilyn Burns.
All rights reserved. Published by Scholastic Inc.
HELLO READER!, CARTWHEEL BOOKS, and the CARTWHEEL BOOKS logo are registered trademarks of Scholastic Inc.

Library of Congress Cataloging-in-Publication Data is available.

12 11 10 9 8 7 6 5   6 7 8 9/9 0/0

Printed in the U.S.A.   24

First Scholastic printing, October 1995

Slower Than a Snail

by Anne Schreiber
Illustrated by Larry Daste

Hello Math Reader — Level 2

SCHOLASTIC INC.
Cartwheel
·B·O·O·K·S·®

New York Toronto London Auckland Sydney

"Hurry up! You're slower than a snail!"

"Slower than a snail?
No way!" I wailed.

"I'm smaller than an elephant.
I'm bigger than a poodle.

I'm shorter than a rocket ship.
I'm longer than a noodle.

I'm wider than a string bean.
I'm narrower than a truck.

I'm lighter than a ton of bricks.

I'm heavier than a duck.

Skyscrapers rise above me.
Tunnels are below.
It's easy to size things up.
I just use what I know!

I'm longer than a shoelace.
I'm shorter than this guy.

I'm smaller than an airplane.
I'm bigger than a fly.

I'm taller than a monkey.
I'm shorter than a tree.

I'm smaller than a rainbow.
I'm bigger than a flea.

I'm larger than some things.
I'm smaller than others.
But there is one thing
I am not, my big brother . . .

and that's slower
than a snail."

• ABOUT THE ACTIVITIES •

Sorting, comparing, and classifying objects in different ways is valuable preparation for children learning about number, measurement, and shape. Children are interested in investigating objects and naturally compare them. For example, they may classify things by whether they are big or little. "That glass is little." "My doll is big." "The package is too big for me to carry."

Later, children become aware of different physical properties of objects. Their observations and comparisons become more precise as they look for relationships between objects. "Your glass holds more than mine." "My doll is taller than yours." "The package is too heavy for me."

The activities and games in this section build on the comparisons made in the story. Some use pictures; some use common objects you might have on hand. The directions are written for you to read along with your child.

Children may enjoy doing their favorite activities again and again. Encourage them to do so. Or try a different activity at each reading. Be open to your child's interests, and have fun with math!

— Marilyn Burns

You'll find tips and suggestions
for guiding the activities whenever
you see a box like this!

Retelling the Story

The little girl said she was smaller than an elephant. You are, too. What other animals are you smaller than?

The girl also said she was bigger than a poodle. Are you? What else are you bigger than?

Reread the story. Think of other things that could be in it.

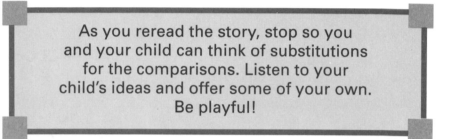

As you reread the story, stop so you and your child can think of substitutions for the comparisons. Listen to your child's ideas and offer some of your own. Be playful!

A Sorting Box

Collect objects and put them in a box.

Try to collect about 20 objects. They can all be the same, such as buttons or keys. Or you can combine objects — buttons, keys, nails, jar lids, nuts, bolts, coins, pebbles, etc. Let your child examine the objects and play with them. Then introduce the sorting activities.

Pick out one object from the box. Tell just one thing about it. You might say that it is round or white or bumpy or something else. But tell just one thing.

Take out all the other objects in the box that are round or white or bumpy or whatever. Put them in a pile.

Then put everything back in the box and play again with another object.

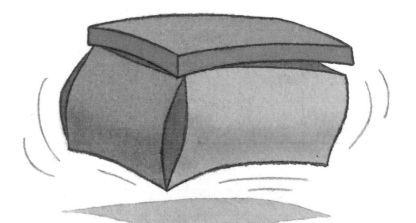

Point to something near the girl.

Point to something far from the girl.

Point to something on top of the girl.

Point to something underneath the girl.

Point to something smaller than the girl.

Point to something larger than the girl.

Point to something taller than the girl.

Point to something shorter than the girl.

What Do I See?

Find picture pairs to solve the riddles.

I see something long, something short.
I see something round, something square.
I see something that is big, something little.
I see something that is tall, something short.
I see something that is wide, something thin.

Can you make up other picture-pair riddles?